this Book belongs to:

Note to the reader: The books in the Max, Annie and Tak series are based on the real life adventures of three English Springer Spaniels. You may notice that Annie is drawn with three legs, and this is because five years ago Annie lost her front leg to cancer. She has survived and is portrayed in the book just as she is, a beautiful and spirited tri-paw.

On a sunny day in May
Max and Annie went out to play.
Max ran like **crazy** around his yard
And dug in the garden long and hard,

Making a hole to **bury** his bone,
Three pairs of glasses and his mom's cell phone.
Annie **strolled** around and **sniffed** all the flowers,
Then lay down and napped in the warm sun for hours.

Both dogs were happy, **content** with their life.
Little did they know, there soon would be **strife!**

At that very moment, in a town close by
A little puppy waited, so **cute** and **shy.**

He had been **adopted** by a nice family,
And he wondered how his life would be.

Would he be **welcomed** with hugs and a smile?
Here comes his new mom, we'll know in awhile.

My name is **Max** and I'm mad and I'm sad.
What could make me feel so bad?

Mom brought home a puppy named "baby" **TAK.**
I want her to take him **back!**

All the neighbors have come by today,
To bring him **treats** and watch him play.

Everyone **kisses** him on his cute little nose,
But I say, get out the hose!

He **smells funny** and looks **different** too.
Why, he can't even chew a **decent** shoe!

Sure, **he's cute** with his fur white and black,
But I want mom to take him back!

And Annie, my **adorable**, big sis,
I can't believe you're putting up with this?

He's taking over; he's moving in,
He's getting all the **attention** and making mom grin.

This can't be good, things are looking black!
I need mom to **take him back!**

What—what's that you say?

Oh no, he's here to stay!

Well, if this pup is going to live with us,
Disrupt my house, and make a fuss,

Instead of going to **obedience** schools,
This puppy has to learn **my rules!**

Tak, come over and **sit down** here,
While I make the house rules perfectly clear.

No playing with my toys, **no** sleeping in my bed,
No eating from my dish, wait for me to be fed.

No sitting in my chair, **no** watching my TV,
No begging for treats or being **cuter** than me.

No being a good boy, that's not the way it goes.
Around here, being **naughty** keeps mom on her toes.

No being **neat** and **orderly**; attack their shoes and clothes.
Nobody minds chewed up mittens, hats and pantyhose.

Now let's move out to the backyard.
You'll find my **outdoor rules** aren't hard.

No playing with my football or any of my toys.
When I'm **napping** in my bushes, don't make any noise.

No barking at the mailman or the girls from UPS.
Protecting the house and **barking** are my jobs, I **confess.**

No sitting in my dog house, even in the rain,
No digging in my garden, no being a **little pain.**

No chewing on my sticks or even on my bone,
Don't forget, this yard is a **puppy-free zone.**

No chasing any of my cat friends up and around our tree,
And for goodness sake, you must stop **following** me!

Now here are my **rules** of the **car** and the **woods**.
Do as I say, do as you should.

No taking my seat when we go for a ride,
No sitting in Annie's seat, **no** sitting by my side.

No sticking your head out the window for air,
No crying and whining that the rules aren't fair.

When we get to the woods, there will be a lot to see,
But you can't get out of the car before me.

In the woods it will be **tempting** to run and play,
But here are the rules. **Don't get carried away!**

No playing, **no** chasing even one forest critter.
All that's my job. You be a **good sitter.**

Just **stay** behind and **camp out** by the car.
Mom won't want you to go very far.

I'm the explorer, the **king** of forest and bog;
I'm one **awesome** hunting dog!

With all that said, Max took off with great speed,
Leaving poor Tak and old Annie **feeling sad,** indeed.

There were **so many rules,** it could make your head spin.

Who could remember them or even begin

To follow the rules laid down by **"mad Max."**

Let's see what Annie sees as the facts.

Annie **smiled** at the **puppy** and said something kind,
Don't listen to Max, pay him no mind.

He's **jealous** because you're so cute and new,
To him you're worse than a case of the flu.

He used to be mom's only boy,
Now you're here to give us joy.

Max needs to **share** the **love** and the kibble.
His rules are mean; they are a bunch of **drivel.**

Listen closely to me, **my rules** are just three.
Follow these and you'll fit into the family.

Rule number one: It's important to come when mom calls your name.
You need to be safe and show mom you're tame.

Eeeek!

(Don't be like Max who comes if he wants,
Especially if he's in one of his favorite **haunts.**
If his head's in a hole, if he's chasing a mole,
Or if he sees a deer, he **pretends** he can't hear!)

Rule number two: Be patient with Max.
Ignore his silly rules and talking attacks.

Max has a **good heart;** he'll wake up soon
And realize a little brother is a really big **boon.**
He'll have someone to play with, a **buddy,** a **pal,**
For running after Max, I'm too old a gal!

Rule number three: Be yourself, be a star.
Explore, sniff around, just don't go too far.

Know your family **loves you** and wants you to grow
Into a dog not afraid to go

Have **fun, splash, run** and **play.**
Learn to **enjoy** every doggie day.

My fur is soft and black and wavy.
I am all brand new, I'm only a **baby.**

I just arrived at my great new home,
And from my mommy, I never will **roam.**

I have a **big sister** whose name is Annie;
She **loves** and **cuddles** me and says she's my grannie.

But the dog I want most to love me is Max.
He's my **big brother,** and right now he acts

As if I'm a **pest,** a **bother,** a **pain.**
If he could, he'd leave me out in the rain.

He made **a list** of rule after rule.
I can't do anything except **sit** and **drool.**

I want to **wrestle, run** and **play,**
Have fun and **grow up,** day by day.

I think what I'll do is **follow Max** around,
Do what he does, stay close to the ground.

When he runs this way, I'll **pounce**, I'll **jump!**
I'll coax him to play and not be a grump.

Anyone can see my brother Max is so **cool.**
He'll see that I'm fun; he's no fool.

Quick here he comes, I'm **jumping** in the air!
I'm so **excited** to see him, I knock over a chair!

Max you're so **terrific,** so handsome, so great,
So **adventurous,** so funny, **best dog** in the state!

I bet you can show me just what to do
So I can be a **great Springer like you!**

Wow, the kid is in **awe** of me, my heart's about to melt!
I had no idea that this is how little Tak felt.

Being a big brother may have its **perks.**
The kid adores me; that's how it works!

I guess I'd better set a **good example**,
    Play with him, **share** and let him sample

The chicken I just took off the kitchen table.
    The kid needs **direction** and a TV with cable.

I'm just the **big brother** that this **little pup** needs.
We'll dig in the garden and plant the seeds

Of a **family** who loves and **appreciates** each other,
Wise sister, little Tak and his **fabulous** big brother!

You might want to know what became of Max's rules.
They were **shredded** and **dragged** through puddles and pools.

Max **discovered** that a lot of rules weren't a good thing:
New brothers, new **playmates** can make your **heart sing.**

From then on the house was filled with **barks** and **laughter**,
And we all **played** and **lived happily** ever after.

MAX

THE END

Big Max

Joe Miller
copyright 2004

verse: G7   a minor   D dom 7   G   D

Max is the King of the cas - tle____ He's the one who makes all the rules____

G   C   a minor   D dom 7   G

Max is big and fast and strong and smart and fun and nev - er wrong Max is real - ly cool____

G
G
chorus: much faster

Max is a big dog big dog big dog Max is a big dog (woof woof!) Max is a big dog big dog big dog

Max is a big dog (woof woof!) (barks loud) (loves mud) (digs holes) (chases squirrels)

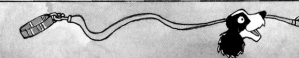

Verse 2:
Tak had a bit of a problem,
He was just the new kid in town.
Small and cute and curious, his playing made Max furious.
Tak smiled upside down . . . felt sad . . . stayed home . . . alone.

Chorus:
Tak is a <u>little</u> dog, <u>little</u> dog, <u>little</u> dog . . . (continue like first chorus)

Verse 3:
Max taught Tak all his rules
Just to keep him out of his way.
"Don't do this and don't do that, don't even think to chase a cat."
Tak couldn't even play . . . or bark . . . or sing . . . or anything.

Chorus:
Max is a <u>bossy</u> dog, <u>bossy</u> dog, <u>bossy</u> dog . . .

Verse 4:
Annie is a smart little princess.
She can smile every day.
She told Tak to never mind, cuz Max would soon be cool and kind.
Annie was always that way . . . nice words . . . big help . . . okay.

Chorus:
Annie is a <u>smart</u> dog, <u>smart</u> dog, <u>smart</u> dog . . .

Verse 5:
So Tak tried to get Max to like him,
Secretly he followed him around.
He'd joke and laugh and pounce and run so Max and he
could have some fun.
A hero he had found . . . cool Max . . . big bro . . . hope so!

Chorus:
Tak is a <u>cute</u> dog, <u>cute</u> dog, <u>cute</u> dog . . .

Verse 6:
Now Tak and Max are like brothers,
And Annie makes a family of three.
Hunting, swimming, digging, fishing, sleeping, playing even wishing
They are all happy . . . have fun . . . play nice . . . bark loud . . .

Chorus:
Max and Tak and Annie are <u>family</u>, <u>family</u> . . .

Add your own lyrics! Think up words that describe Max, Tak and Annie, and use your words
in place of the underlined words in the **chorus,** or add your own descriptions at the end of each **verse.**

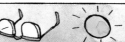

 # Let's Write

Why was Max so upset when the new puppy, Tak, arrived?

Have you ever had a new baby (or a new family member) join your family? How did you feel when he or she moved in?

What rules would you make up for your new family member?

Pretend you are Max. What rules, not in the story, would you make up for the puppy?

How did Annie help Tak feel welcome in his new family?

Why did Max change his mind and decide to play with Tak?

List some good things about having a new brother/sister, or family member.

Readers' Theater

The use of different voices in **Max's Rules** lends itself perfectly to a readers' theater presentation. The beginning of the book may be assigned to a narrator. Then each participant can take the part of a different dog, "mad" Max, sensible, Annie and the "baby" Tak. Conveniently the book is divided into three separate sections, one for each character and concludes with a choral reading. The end pages also contain a rousing song complete with sheet music. Only a few basic props are needed: an easel, doggie toys, bones, a dog bed and such. Simple costumes could be made from white shirts colored with brown and black spots and dog ears stapled to a headband.

This activity would be appropriate for the classroom, assemblies, library/media centers, youth groups, drama clubs and for those who like to put on plays at home. Have fun!

Rhyming Fun

Sandy, Max, Annie and Tak love to play with words and make rhymes. This book was written in **rhyming couplets** where the last word in each of two sentences rhymes. An example is:

No taking my seat when we go for a **ride**,
No sitting in Annie's seat, no sitting by my **side.**

Can you make up some rhyming couplets?*

Max is a dog who is usually _____,
But when he saw the puppy, he got _____.

Tak is cute and funny and _____,
Except when he jumps with dirty _____!

Annie is smart, funny and _____;
You can see her wisdom in her big brown _____.

You can also try to write a limerick.

The rhyming lines are 1 & 2, 3 & 4, and 5 rhymes with 1 & 2. An example is:

1. Here are Max, Annie and **Tak,**

2. Three dogs who love to **snack.**

3. They like chicken and **rice,**

4. And beef is real **nice.**

5. But gummy worms make their lips **smack!**

Now you try one . . .

*glad / mad / sweet / feet / wise / eyes

Word fun

Max's Rules has lots of good words in it. Most of them you can figure out as you read, but some of them you can look up in the dictionary. See if you can write your own sentences using the following words. Rhyme if you want to!

content	zone	haunt
strife	tempting	roam
adorable	awesome	pounce
disrupt	Jealous	adventurous
obedience	drivel	perks
confess	ignore	appreciate

Thank You to our Schools

The mission of the **Chagrin River Publishing Company** is to give children, teachers, librarians and parents a voice in what is published for them. The author, Sandra Philipson, visited many schools this past school year, and during the visits she listened to everyone's ideas for **Max's Rules.** Many classes, as part of the Max and Annie educational program, contributed their thoughts about what Max's rules should be and even how the story should end. Using the children's suggestions as a starting point, Mrs. Philipson created this book. More than 10,000 children from the schools listed below contributed to this project. We at Chagrin River Publishing Company want to thank all the children, teachers, librarians, principals and dog walkers who helped us create **Max's Rules.**

Avon East Elementary School

Bellestone Elementary School

Bethlehem Elementary School

Bissell Elementary School

Buckeye Woods Elementary School

Cardinal Middle School

Conesville Elementary School

Craddock Elementary School

Crosby Elementary School

Cottage Grove Elementary School

Cuyahoga Heights Elementary School

Dodge Middle School

Drake Elementary School

Elm Grove Elementary School

Ford Middle School

Forest Elementary School

Goshen Center Elementary School

Green High School

Harmon Elementary School

Hopewell Elementary School

Huntsburg Elementary School

Hylen Souders Elementary School

Lake Cable Elementary School

Lakeland Elementary School

Lemoyne Elementary School

Lewis Elementary School

Lincoln Elementary School

Longcoy Elementary School

Luckey Elementary School

Madison Elementary School

Maple Elementary School

Murlin Heights Elementary School

Max Larsen Elementary School

Park Elementary School

Parkside Elementary School

Pemberville Elementary School

Pleasant Valley Elementary School

Powers Elementary School

Reed Middle School

Richie Elementary School

Roosevelt Elementary School

Sauder Elementary School

St. Peter's Elementary School

Toth Elementary School

Turkey Foot Elementary School

Villa Montessori School

Warwood Elementary School

Webster Elementary School

Westfall Elementary School

West Liberty Elementary School

Woodsdale Elementary School

The Real Max, Annie and Tak

Photograph by: Amy Sancetta

Max

Max is now 7 years old. These days he spends a lot of time visiting children in schools with Annie, Tak and his mom, Sandy Philipson. In the last five years, the dogs have been to more than 240 schools, and Max has escaped from 24 of them! He has jumped over fences, bolted out open doors, pulled away from dog walkers and dug tunnels under playground equipment. He does other naughty things too. At one school he dug up their spring flowers; at another, he jumped in their fish tank; and a few times he terrorized school pets such as gerbils, butterflies, frogs, fish, hamsters, and bunnies. Max is a sweet guy, but his desire to hunt can get him into lots of trouble, especially in school. As you might imagine, he has trouble sitting still!

Annie, the three-legged Springer, is now 14 years old. (Annie has survived the cancer that caused her to lose her front leg five years ago.) She also spends lots of time visiting schools as she is not yet ready to retire. Annie became a movie star last year when **"Miracle Dogs,"** her family film, premiered on Animal Planet. The movie is based on her book, **<u>Annie Loses Her Leg but Finds Her Way</u>** and emphasizes the sometimes magical relationship between animals and the people who love them.

Tak is the latest addition to Max and Annie's family. He is 18 months old and is still an energetic puppy. He loves to play with Max, tackling him every chance he gets. Like most puppies, he can sometimes be a pest. He likes to eat the covers off paperback books; he chews glasses, shoes, notebooks and anything he can steal off the kitchen counter. Tak is very affectionate and always cuddly. Like Max and Annie,

Photograph by: Amy Sancetta

Tak

Photograph by: Amy Sancetta

Annie

he is a registered therapy dog, and he is always ready to give someone a snuggle to make them feel better. He travels everywhere with Max and Annie, and this year he visited over 50 schools. He also loves being the "star" of **Max's Rules.**

Max, Annie and Tak have traveled a lot in the last five years, but their favorite places to visit besides schools and libraries, are hospitals and/or events for children and families touched by cancer. All the dogs hope that they bring some comfort to both

grownups and children with their friendly ways and doggie kisses.

Other books in the Max and Annie series are: **Annie Loses Her Leg but Finds Her Way**, **Max's Wild Goose Chase**, **The Artist**, and **Max and Annie's Mysterious Campfire.**

You can visit Max, Annie and Tak on their website at www.maxandannie.com.

photo album